For my Mama.
—D. P.

Library of Congress Cataloging-in-Publication Data available.

ISBN 978-1-7972-0282-2

Manufactured in China.

 MIX
Paper from responsible sources
FSC www.fsc.org   FSC™ C008047

Design by Lydia Ortiz.
Typeset in Recoleta.

The illustrations in this book were rendered in gouache, watercolor, and colored pencil.

10 9 8 7 6 5 4 3 2 1

Chronicle books and gifts are available at special quantity discounts to corporations, professional associations, literacy programs, and other organizations. For details and discount information, please contact our premiums department at corporatesales@chroniclebooks.com or at 1-800-759-0190.

Chronicle Books LLC
680 Second Street
San Francisco, California 94107

Chronicle Books—we see things differently. Become part of our community at www.chroniclekids.com.

The Fox and the Forest Fire

Danny Popovici

chronicle books·san francisco

I wasn't sure I'd like my new home.

Nights are too quiet.

Mornings are too loud.

I hike with my mom.

My pack gets tangled, I trip over rocks,
and a bug flies into my mouth, twice.
"I don't like this place!"

In time, I discover there are a lot of things to do in the forest.

I study bugs and the plants that house them.

I build rock dams where small fish can rest.

And there are new
friends to meet.

"Oh, you play here, too?"

I feel welcome in my new home.

Then one morning,
it's strangely quiet.

I see a plume of smoke
off in the distance.

I hurry to warn my mother.

And I wonder if we will ever
see our home again.

Even after a late-season rain,
we have to wait a long time
before we're allowed to go home.

Our house is gone,

but we are safe.

While things don't look like they did before,
the forest knows what to do after a fire.

And so do we.

Author's Note

One summer many years ago, I had an opportunity to be a part of a forest firefighting crew. It was only then that I learned to appreciate spending time in the woods, surrounded by nature and animals, able to see thousands of stars. Until that point, as a city dweller like our main character (whom I call Oswald), I hadn't even been camping! Everything changed that summer as a new world opened to me, right in my own backyard. Even though I no longer fight fires, I still spend a lot of time in the forest, hiking, camping, and looking for a good lake to take a swim with my dog.

More recently, an uncontrolled forest fire raged through the gorge (an area between large hills) near my home. The air was so smoky, we had to stay inside. I couldn't help but think of the forest animals, their homes, and where they could go to be safe. Because the smoke and fire endangered their homes, they had to flee closer to the city, often finding themselves in residential backyards. No longer a part of the forest fire-fighting crew, there was very little I could do, so I decided to write and illustrate the book that you're holding right now.

More about Wildfires

Wildfires are an unsettling sight, especially when they get close to communities of people. Like Oswald and his mother, it's important to get as far away from a fire as possible and let the firefighters handle the situation. But it's good to remember, while a burned forest doesn't look like it once did, it will rebuild itself. It might be hard to believe, but in the right conditions, a naturally occurring forest fire can actually benefit the forest by helping it grow bigger and stronger than before.

When fires occur naturally, they can help eliminate excess debris and decay from forest floors. That overgrowth can prevent some animals and organisms from accessing the important nutrients and sunlight they need to thrive. Fires also clear out invasive species that compete for nutrients that could sustain a healthier native habitat.

Forest managers try to reduce overgrowth and invasive species while preventing wildfires from endangering communities by allowing controlled burns that are monitored by trained professionals.

Still, too many wildfires are caused inadvertently, by human activity. Wildfires are also made more common by extreme weather and our changing climate, so it's vital that we take action to protect our environment in order to ensure thriving, healthy forests for generations to come.